Absolutely
Beastly
Children

Absolutely Beastly Children

by Dan Krall

TRICYCLE PRESS
Berkeley

A is for Andy

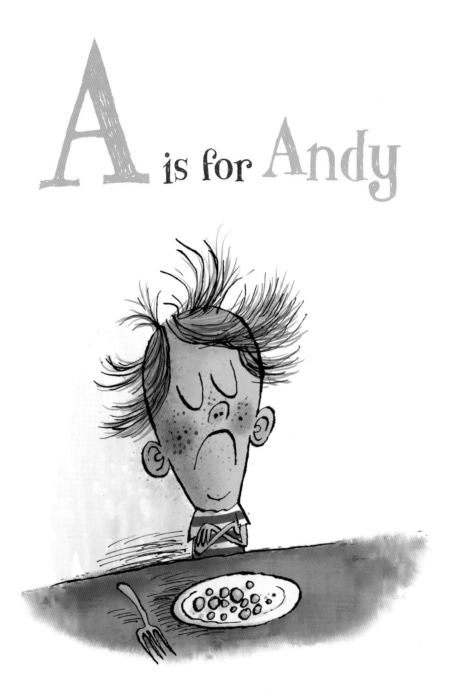

who won't eat his peas.

B

is for

Becky

who cannot
say please.

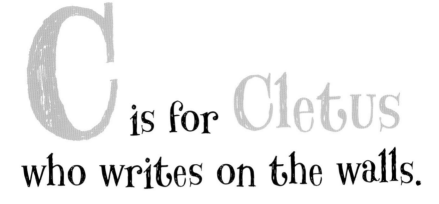

C is for Cletus
who writes on the walls.

D is for Deon
who won't come when
he's called.

E is for Esther.

She won't wash her hands.

F is for Florence,
the Queen of Demands.

G is for Gertrude

who stays up too late.

H is for Hameed
who won't wash his plate.

I is for Isaac

who cries all the time.

J is for Jeffrey.

He knows how to whine.

K is for Kathy

who won't brush her teeth.

 **L**
is for
Linda
who won't
wash her
feet.

M is for Martha
who belongs in a zoo.

N is for Nancy

who plays with her food.

is for
Oscar
who likes
to tell lies.

P is for Percy.

He pulls wings off flies.

Q is for Quincy

who teases the cat.

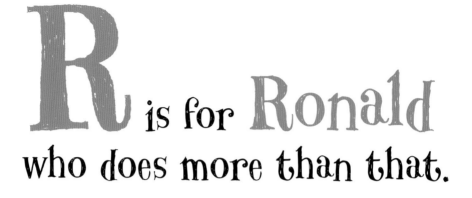

R is for Ronald
who does more than that.

S is for Sigmund
who still wets the bed.

T is for Tara who won't brush her head.

U is for Ursula
who gets into fights.

V

is for
Violet
who does
nothing
right.

W is for Wendy.

She's very loud.

X 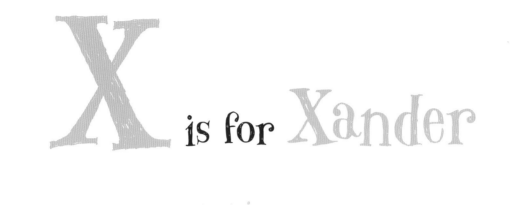 is for Xander

who farts in a crowd.

Y

is for

Yoshi

whose parents aren't proud.

Z is for Zachary,
the worst of the bunch.

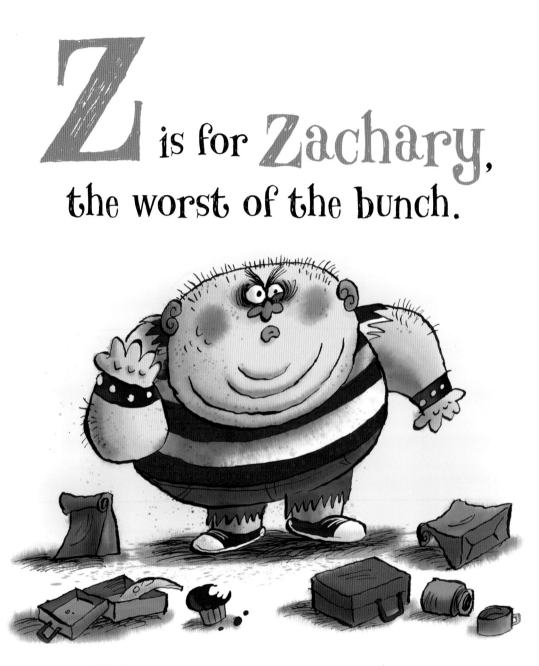

He beats them all up
and steals their lunch.

All rights reserved. Published in the United States by Tricycle Press, an imprint of
Random House Children's Books, a division of Random House, Inc., New York.
www.randomhouse.com/kids
www.tricyclepress.com

Tricycle Press and the Tricycle Press colophon are registered trademarks of
Random House, Inc.

Library of Congress Cataloging-in-Publication Data

Krall, Dan.
  Absolutely beastly children / by Dan Krall. — 1st ed.
     p. cm.
  Summary: A rhyming alphabet of children behaving poorly, from Andy,
who will not eat his peas to Zachary, who beats up all the other
children and steals their lunches.
[1. Stories in rhyme. 2. Behavior—Fiction. 3. Alphabet.] I. Title.
  PZ8.3.K86Ab 2010
  [E]—dc22
                              2009051620

ISBN 978-1-58246-333-9 (hardcover)
ISBN 978-1-58246-365-0 (Gibraltar lib. bdg.)

Printed in China

Design by Betsy Stromberg
Typeset in Hombre and Paperback
The illustrations in this book were created digitally.

1 2 3 4 5 6 — 14 13 12 11 10

First Edition